LADYBIRD BOOKS, INC.
Lewiston, Maine 04240 U.S.A.
© LADYBIRD BOOKS LTD MCMLXXXVII
Loughborough, Leicestershire, England

Printed in England

# Hansel and Gretel

written by HY MURDOCK
illustrated by BRUCE WAITE

Ladybird Books

Once upon a time, a woodcutter and his wife lived in a cottage on the edge of the forest. The woodcutter had two children—a boy named Hansel and a girl named Gretel.

But the woodcutter's wife, who was the children's stepmother, didn't like children. The family was very poor and they were often hungry.

One night, when their food was nearly gone, the stepmother said, ''We must take the children into the forest and leave them.''

The woodcutter was sad. He loved his children—but there was no food for them, and so he agreed.

Hansel and Gretel were so hungry that they lay awake in bed. They had heard what their stepmother had said. Gretel began to cry.

"Don't cry," said Hansel. "I'll save us."

He crept outside and quietly filled his pockets with small, white pebbles, which shone in the moonlight.

The next morning, their stepmother gave Hansel and Gretel some bread to take with them. The family set off into the forest, but Hansel walked slowly behind, dropping pebbles from his pocket.

Deep in the forest the woodcutter made a fire for his children and told them to stay by it. "We shall come back for you," he said.

Hansel and Gretel ate their bread, and soon they went to sleep by the fire. When they woke, it was dark and they were afraid. Then Hansel said, "I can find the way back. I left a trail of pebbles! Look how they shine in the moonlight!"

The woodcutter was pleased to see them, but their stepmother was very angry that they had found their way home.

It was not long before the stepmother made the woodcutter promise again that he would leave Hansel and Gretel in the forest. The children heard, but this time the door was locked and Hansel couldn't creep out to collect any pebbles.

The next day, Hansel and Gretel took their pieces of bread, and the woodcutter led them even deeper into the forest. Hansel walked slowly behind.

The woodcutter made a fire and again left Hansel and Gretel in the forest. They went to sleep and did not wake up until it was dark.

They knew that they were lost, but Hansel told Gretel that he had left a trail of breadcrumbs so that they could find their way back.

They searched in the moonlight but couldn't find the trail. The birds who lived in the forest had eaten Hansel's crumbs.

In the morning, the children wandered in the forest again. Suddenly they found a very strange cottage, made from all sorts of delicious things—cookies, cakes, peppermint sticks, chocolate...

They were so hungry that they broke off pieces to eat.

Then out came an ugly woman who said in a cackling voice, ''My dears! You are lost. Come and stay with me. I will give you food and look after you.''

The children were afraid, but they went inside. They didn't know that this old woman was really a wicked witch who liked to eat children.

But they soon found out!

The witch locked Hansel in a cage. ''I shall feed you until you are nice and fat, and then I shall cook you in the oven,'' she cackled.

Every day the witch asked Hansel to poke his finger through the bars of the cage so that she could feel how fat he was. But clever Hansel held out a stick instead of his finger, and the witch, who couldn't see very well, didn't know why he still felt so thin.

One morning the witch was tired of waiting. She made Gretel make a big fire in the oven. Then the witch told her to climb inside to see if it was hot enough. But Gretel said, ''Perhaps you could get inside and see for yourself.''

As soon as the witch climbed into the oven, Gretel slammed the door shut.

Gretel ran to let Hansel out of the cage. The children found jewels in the witch's cottage. Now they were rich!

When they returned home, they found that their stepmother had gone. The woodcutter was overjoyed to see his children, and they all lived happily ever after.